CW00919441
Penguin Oil
Penguin Oil

SEA GEM

and

the Land of Ice

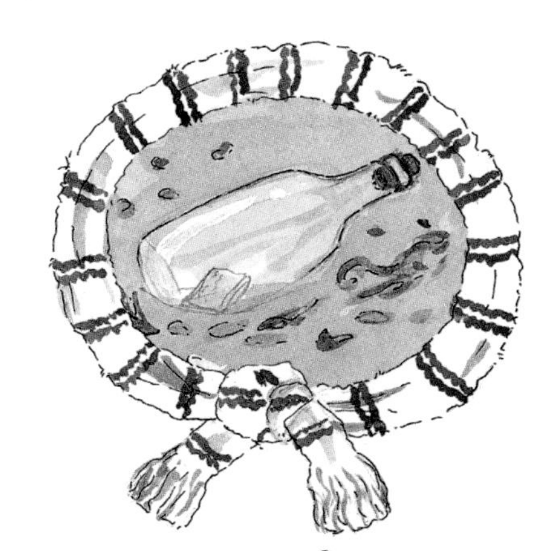

Annie O'Dowd

When you see this hat
in the story, turn to Captain Hail's Miscellanea
(or a Guide to Life in the Land of Ice) on page 72.

1
Sea Gem's Daydream

FOAMY BAY IS A VERY WARM PLACE. In summer, the bright sun shimmers above the scorching sand and flashes on the sea like sharp glass. Under the hot sky, swarms of insects gather in the drowsy haze and plants wilt. Sea Gem hated the heat. Unlike her brothers and sisters, who could cool off in the bubbly surf, Sea Gem had to stay indoors or sit under the trees wearing a large hat. This was because she was a rare white seadog who couldn't go into the hot sun. If she did, her pale skin was bound to get horribly burnt. When the temperature rose, Sea Gem languished in the shade and imagined herself in a cold place where the sun couldn't harm her.

Sea Gem's twin brother, Tumblegrass, was an ordinary brown seadog. In fact, none of Sea Gem's brothers and sisters was white like her, and in her gloomier moods, Sea Gem thought she had been born into the wrong family altogether. That's probably why she seemed a very quiet and shy seadog. But how we appear on the outside is not always the whole picture. For instance, when Sea Gem told an exciting story, she forgot her shyness and her little white face became a mirror of each thrilling moment. She recounted many such gripping chronicles to me; some fact, some pure fantasy. But of all of the tales she told, none was as incredible as the one which happened to Sea Gem herself. I'm not sure you'll believe it, but every word is true. She was only halfway past her first birthday (that's ten in human years) when she went on a brave journey far from home, all the way to the bottom of the world! Although I cannot do the special voices like Sea Gem does, I will try my best to remember all of the exciting bits.

The story begins in the quiet village of Foamy Bay on a hot summer afternoon. Sea Gem was sitting with Tumblegrass under a large tree in the cool shelter of a sandbank. She scanned the shoreline for her parents and saw her mother, Blue Bottle, standing at the water's edge holding the new twins, Cotton Reel and Tangle. She caught sight of her father at the wheel of the family boat. Old Cork shouted instructions to the older children, who were helping him to trim the sails.

Some of the other boats were already at sea, moving across the foam-capped waves, their sails pillowy against the sky.

'You'd better hurry,' Sea Gem said to her twin. 'I think they're ready to leave.'

'I wish you could come too,' replied Tumblegrass. Sea Gem shook her head.

'Don't worry,' she said, 'I'm going to practise my harp.' She picked up the instrument then, and began to play.

'You really don't mind?' he asked. Sea Gem didn't reply, but plucked the strings in soft chords. Without a moment's hesitation, Tumblegrass ran down the beach towards the water, shouting, 'Father! Wait for me!'

Sea Gem sadly watched his retreating form. Presently, Blue Bottle came walking towards her, carrying the babies. Tangle was barking.

'Hello, Sea Gem,' her mother said as she approached. 'We're off for a nap.'

Sea Gem nodded.

'Stay in the shade,' Blue Bottle added before continuing back to the burrow.

Sea Gem was alone. She knew it was silly, but she felt hot tears blur her eyes. Ugly blue eyes; ugly white fur! To everyone else she was a very pretty seadog, as delicate and pale as a ghost gum flower. Sadly, Sea Gem thought that she was a freak. After all, everyone stared at her wherever she went. As well as that, she was always missing out on things the rest of the family was doing, especially in summer.

And it wasn't just her colour that was peculiar. Ever since she was a tiny baby, she had been troubled by daydreams. They happened without warning. She would hear a whooshing sound in her ears and then she would see things, things that weren't there. Sometimes she saw events before they happened, or had visions of scenes from the past. She had even known about her sister Marigold being found as a baby in a basket at sea before anyone told her. She'd seen it one day in a vivid daydream when she'd picked up Marigold's glasses. The vision had

been so real that it had frightened her; and afterwards she'd been tired and drained, and had had to be put to bed with a cup of squink.

Sitting on the beach, Sea Gem was adjusting her hat and trying to banish the sad thoughts when something glinted with a quick flash. She scanned the shoreline. Then she saw it again, lying on the dark sand where the tide had retreated. Sea Gem moved towards it, and when she came close, she saw it was a bottle with a cork in the top. Through the greenish glass, she could see a folded note!

Sea Gem picked the bottle up. But as soon as she touched it, there was a whooshing sound in her ears. It gave her a hollow feeling; a sick feeling as if she were being turned inside out. She staggered as dizziness nearly overcame her. Then, in the very next moment, she was no longer on the beach. This wasn't just an ordinary daydream. Around her, gigantic icebergs sailed silently, their frozen shadows turning the sea dark blue. The air was sharp and as clear as the cleanest thing you could imagine. Then, the vision began to fade. It grew transparent, but before it vanished altogether, a face appeared. It came into focus for a moment and then was gone. Sea Gem, once more, was standing on the beach, holding the bottle in her paw. In another wave of dizziness, Sea Gem fainted. She collapsed on the sand, and her hat rolled off.

2
A Message from the Land of Ice

LATER, WHEN THE afternoon sun was making long shadows, Blue Bottle found Sea Gem lying near the water's edge. In her paw she clutched the strange bottle.

'Sea Gem?' said Blue Bottle, her voice tight with alarm. The little seadog whimpered as she woke up. One side of her face was badly sunburned, as were two of her paws.

'Oh no, sunburn!' her mother exclaimed. She took the bottle and helped Sea Gem to her feet.

Back at the burrow, Blue Bottle dabbed a solution of mangrove bark gently onto Sea Gem's sunburn.

'What happened?' she asked.

'I'm not sure,' Sea Gem replied, flinching. 'I felt so dizzy … and then …'

Sea Gem's story was interrupted by barking. The rest of the family had returned.

'Hello, Sea Gem, I caught eleven fish!' shouted Tumblegrass as he bounded into the bed-snug.

'Sea Gem has bad sunburn,' Blue Bottle said. 'Why don't you sit with her for a while?'

Sea Gem tried to smile at her twin, but her face hurt to move.

'Will she be all right?' asked Tumblegrass anxiously.

'She'll be fine in a day or so,' Blue Bottle replied with a smile. Then she hurried out to prepare the dinner.

Tumblegrass sat on the edge of Sea Gem's bed. 'What's this?' he asked, picking up the greenish bottle.

'I found it on the beach,' Sea Gem replied, trying not to think about the weird daydream she had had.

'Look, Sea Gem,' said Tumblegrass, peering into the bottle, 'it's a message!'

'Yes,' replied Sea Gem, remembering the folded piece of paper.

Tumblegrass prised out the cork and shook the note onto the bed. Then he carefully opened it. It was a hand-drawn picture of a boy seadog. *Lost*, said the curly writing at the top. There was some more writing underneath the picture, but it

was very difficult to read as the ink had been damaged by water. *'Please ... help me ... alone ... Fr ... a ... y* something ...' Tumblegrass read slowly. After that it was harder to decipher, and he held the note closer to the light.

Sea Gem gasped in recognition. It was the place she had seen in her vision. A small picture of icebergs and the words *Land of Ice* were faintly traced on the bottom of the piece of paper. There was another thing, too; the seadog in the picture reminded her of someone she knew.

That night while Sea Gem slept, she dreamed again of the Land of Ice. She saw the icebergs and then the same face. She saw that it was the face of the seadog on the note and he spoke in a strange accent.

'I've turned those cheeses. Shall I see to the orphans?'

It was such a funny thing to say that Sea Gem woke up. It was already morning, and a bright stripe of sunlight lay across her bed. She felt the tightness of the sunburn, but it wasn't as bad as before. How she hated the sun! She wished she lived in a cold place where the sun couldn't hurt her. Sea Gem climbed out of bed and headed for the cooking-snug. As she opened the door, the loud clattering and barking told her that everyone was already eating breakfast. She watched quietly from the doorway. Nobody turned and saw her standing there.

'At Choppy Inlet,' Left Shoe was saying between mouthfuls of seed cake, 'there's a ship all the way from the Land of Ice. It's a steamship.'

'Hmmm, a steamship, you say. Why don't we go and have a look today, then?' said Old Cork. 'I'd be interested to meet the captain.'

'Can we come too, Father?' asked Tumblegrass.

'All right,' said Old Cork, chuckling. 'We'll all go, except, of course, for Sea Gem. Sea Gem will have to stay indoors.'

'I've been to the Land of Ice,' Sea Gem said suddenly.

'Sea Gem!' barked Blue Bottle, 'I didn't see you there …'

'I've been to the Land of Ice!' she said again, more loudly this time.

Old Cork and Blue Bottle shared a meaningful glance.

'Now, Sea Gem, I think you mean in your imagination, don't you?' said Blue Bottle.

'I don't know, Mother,' said Sea Gem quietly. 'It felt like I was really there.'

'What did you see?' asked Tumblegrass.

Well,' she said slowly, 'I saw the icebergs … and there was a face. Then I saw the same face again in a dream. He talked strangely.'

'What did he say?' asked Marigold.

'Well …' Sea Gem began, looking uncertain. 'I think he said, *"I've turned those cheeses, shall I see to the orphans?"'*

There was a slight pause as the rest of the Sandburrows tried to look serious. Tumblegrass burst into laughter. 'That's funny!' he barked. Then the rest of the family laughed too.

But Sea Gem wasn't laughing. In fact, she couldn't even smile. She just stood there silently. She felt so ugly. She could feel her horrible pink and white face growing hot with embarrassment. Her eyes stung and she crossly brushed away a tear.

'Come on, Sea Gem,' said Blue Bottle, collecting herself. 'We aren't laughing at you …' But Blue Bottle didn't have time to finish what she was saying, because Sea Gem had turned away and quietly left the room.

I know what you're thinking. You're wondering why the family didn't run after her and make sure she wasn't too upset. But the very next moment, one of the babies dropped a china cup. Old Cork rushed over to clear up the sharp pieces and by the time it was tidied away, everyone had forgotten about Sea Gem. It all might have been different if Sea Gem hadn't gone to her bed-snug and shut the door.

The strange bottle was still standing on her bedside table, and next to it lay the crumpled note. Sea Gem remembered those miserable words, *lost … help … alone.* Her gentle heart was saddened, as she felt alone too. Sea Gem was frightened to touch the sorrowful letter, but she was drawn to it like an insect to a candle flame. She reached out and picked it up. The whooshing sound roared in her ears and once again she was in the Land of Ice. This time, she was standing on the deck of a boat. It had a tall black chimney and made a chugging sound as it moved forwards through an ice-strewn sea. The vision faded and the seadog on the note appeared. His gloomy face seemed to cry out to her. Then he vanished. When she found herself once again standing in her bed-snug, Sea Gem made a decision. She resolved to help the lost boy on the note. She would go to Choppy Inlet and find that boat with the tall black chimney. She would travel to the Land of Ice.

The door opened and Sea Gem jumped. Blue Bottle poked her head through the gap.

'Sea Gem,' she said, 'the others have gone down to Choppy Inlet. I'm going to rest with the babies.' She yawned lengthily and then added, 'Will you be all right?'

'Yes, Mother,' Sea Gem said, tears suddenly springing to her eyes. Once again, her family had gone off without her. She was always alone! Sea Gem sniffed and wiped her face with her sleeve. Then she realised that the house was quiet. No one would notice if she ran away right now, this very moment.

After a rapid search, Sea Gem found a large duffel bag at the back of her cupboard. She pushed the bottle inside. Her heart began to beat faster as her determination grew. She spied the clothes basket in the corner and had a sudden idea. When she had found one of her brother Driftwood's old shirts, and a pair of Tumblegrass' trousers, she put them on and checked her image in the mirror. In Driftwood's sailor shirt she could pass as a cabin boy. Turning around slowly, she inspected her white tail poking out of the wag. No one would recognise her dressed as a boy. She pulled on a woollen cap and hurried off to collect the rest of her supplies. Sea Gem had to be very quiet so as not to alert her mother. When she was ready, she wrote a short note and propped it up against the squink-pot. *Gone to the Land of Ice*, it said in careful printing, *love Sea Gem*. Her heart banged an uneven rhythm. Pulling the cap down to hide her face, she shouldered her duffel bag and walked out the door.

3
The Stowaway

WHEN SEA GEM ARRIVED at Choppy Inlet, it was late afternoon. She made her way to the long jetty, keeping out of sight in case she saw anyone she knew. Carefully checking each boat, Sea Gem searched for the special steamship from the Land of Ice. Then, at the far end of the pier she spotted a different kind of boat. Instead of a mast and sails, this small ship had a tall black chimney. It was the boat she had seen in her dream the night before, the very boat she had been hoping to find.

When she reached its mooring, Sea Gem hid behind a stack of crates to wait for an opportunity to sneak on board. After a while, an unkempt seadog came out on deck. He had the shaggiest fur she had ever seen. She watched as he pulled on a dark blue sailor's cap and then, after another few moments, he disembarked. Sea Gem decided that the shaggy fellow must be the captain. When he had disappeared into the distance, all was quiet. No one else seemed to be about, so she scampered out from behind the crates and onto the deck of the little steamship. Sliding open the hatch, Sea Gem climbed silently inside.

The cosy cabin had a couple of chairs pulled up in front of a small stove. In the corner was a bunk half hidden by a curtain, and beside that a round table covered with a variety of charts and maps. The topmost chart showed the information she had been looking for. The Land of Ice was clearly marked, and a dotted line traced the way northwards to Foamy Bay. Sea Gem gasped with excitement as she followed the direction of its return journey, back to the bottom of the world, to the Land of Ice.

Now that Sea Gem knew for sure that she had the right boat, the next problem was where to hide. After a tense search, she found the entrance to the cargo hold inside the cabin. When she had managed to open its little slatted door, she saw that it was cool and dry inside. This would be a perfect hiding place! She climbed in and retrieved the matches from her bag to light her lantern. Then she inspected the gloomy confines. To her surprise, the hold was full of boxes, sacks and earthenware jars of food.

The LAND of ICE

Sea Gem found herself a comfortable spot next to a sack, and spread out her coat. After a while she heard the sounds of the captain returning. She blew out the lamp and listened. The cool darkness soothed her and in moments she fell into an exhausted sleep. During the night, as Sea Gem slept, the little steamship chugged out of the harbour and onto the open sea.

The next part of Sea Gem's story is quite dull, so I won't bore you with the details. After all, it is a very long way to the Land of Ice. Sea Gem spent most of the time hiding in the hold, and feeling very frightened that she would be discovered. Sometimes, at night, she would sneak out on deck and even occasionally creep into the warmth of the captain's cabin. He was a very heavy sleeper who snored loudly in his bunk behind the curtain. She felt safe enough to sit quietly in the little room while he slept. Often she tidied the cabin or read a book from the captain's small library. She told me she was sometimes very bored, but as each day passed, she felt she was getting closer and closer to the seadog in the note.

One night Sea Gem had been sitting in the little cabin reading quietly when she was startled by a sudden noise. This was followed by a scuffle and a couple of little bangs. Sea Gem realised too late that the captain had woken up, and the curtains around his bunk were opening!

4 Icebergs!

Sea Gem froze, hardly daring to breathe. Then, an unexpected thing happened. The captain greeted her politely with a bow and welcomed her aboard. She noticed that he spoke in a strange accent which was difficult to understand.

'At last, we meet,' he said, smiling. 'I suspected I had a little stowaway on board. I was just waiting for you to show yourself. It's tiresomely lonely on these long journeys and I could do with the help of a cabin boy like you.'

Sea Gem was about to tell the captain that she wasn't a boy at all, but then stopped. Maybe he would think her more useful for the various chores around the little ship if he believed that she was a boy. So instead of telling him the truth, she kept quiet. After that they became good friends. Every day Sea Gem helped to shovel fuel into the furnace to keep the little steamship chugging along, and each night they told each other stories after supper. Their simple meals were of dried fruit, crackers, and wedges of delicious cheese.

In happy companionship they passed the remainder of the long voyage. Sea Gem didn't reveal anything of the note or the bottle, but said only that she wanted to see the Land of Ice.

Soon the weather grew cold and the captain made Sea Gem a bunk in his cabin where she would be warmer and more comfortable. One night, as she was sleeping soundly under her knitted quilts, she had a dream. Actually it wasn't a dream, it was a nightmare.

She was sitting on an ice sheet surrounded by freezing water. Some short distance away on the same piece of ice was another seadog. A boy seadog. He lay with his back towards her. Sea Gem called out to him, and when he turned to face her, she saw that it was the seadog from the note! His eyes were wide with pain and, underneath his leg, a dark bloom of blood spread across the ice. Sea Gem gasped in horror. She tried to move towards him, but the ice platform shifted a little and she lost her balance. Before she had time to comprehend what was happening, a sudden splash erupted from the water beside her and a terrifying creature landed on the ice. It was spotted with a sleek head, and it opened its red mouth wide.

Sea Gem woke up with a start. Her heart was pounding with fright, and it took her a moment to remember where she was. The morning was bitterly cold and the cabin was bathed in a strange grey light. Sea Gem peered through one of the portholes, but it was impossible to see outside. Fog thickened in white tendrils, swirling around the small ship like a cloak.

The captain drew back the curtain sleepily. When he saw the fog, his eyes widened in alarm and, pulling on his warm coat and cap, he moved in the direction of the wheelhouse. Before he opened the hatch, he turned back to Sea Gem.

'Could you keep watch up on deck for me?'

Sea Gem nodded, then asked, 'What must I watch for?'

'Icebergs,' replied the captain grimly.

Up on deck Sea Gem shivered in the freezing air. She peered through the fog, watching for any gaps in the mist that might give her a clear view. The captain had switched the engine to its lowest speed and the little ship chugged steadily forwards. In the next moment, the fog lifted, thinning and opening like ghostly curtains.

'Captain!' Sea Gem barked. 'Iceberg at twelve o'clock!'

Directly ahead of the boat, a massive iceberg blocked their path. The captain waved to Sea Gem from the wheelhouse and turned the boat carefully to portside.

The iceberg was flat-topped and the luminous surface reflected many colours from its depths. The sea-washed sides were worn back in delicate arches, making strange caves. Parts of it glowed bright blue. As they chugged slowly through the ice-choked sea, the frozen lumps made knocking and scraping sounds against the boat. The iceberg's frozen shadow darkened the deck. Sea Gem was silent with awe.

The fog cleared further, revealing land ahead. Tall, snow-covered mountains could be seen in the distance, and in front of their sloping outline was a broad sheet of ice, a shining floor

on the water. It stretched all the way from the boat to an area of shoreline etched in a dark smudge at the foot of the mountains. Sea Gem watched breathlessly as the boat approached. Finally, she had reached the place she had foreseen – the Land of Ice.

The captain turned off the engine and the pistons slowed to a stop with a final blast of steam. Then there was silence. The call of a bird sounded to break the quiet as they prepared to disembark. 'Sea Gem, your paws!' the captain shouted suddenly. 'You have no boots!'

Sea Gem frowned. She had never owned a pair of boots.

'You need to protect your feet from frostbite, Sea Gem,' explained the captain. 'Jump on my back,' he offered, crouching down. 'It's not far and I can easily carry you there.'

She nodded, and the captain lifted her up.

'I'm taking you to my house,' he said. 'My sister lives there with her family, as well as my other relatives … and the orphans.'

'The orphans?' asked Sea Gem. 'Who are the orphans?'

'Why, the orphan penguins, of course,' replied her friend. 'We care for the lost chicks from the penguin colonies.'

The snow squeaked and scrunched with the captain's footsteps, and the cold seemed to increase with each moment. Sea Gem huddled against him and the kind fellow held her feet in his pockets to keep them warm.

Sea Gem noticed that the sky was growing darker and a freezing wind was beginning to blow. They passed a driftwood sign that read *Blueberg Hamlet* and Sea Gem could see a small cluster of dwellings ahead. She was amazed to behold not burrow homes, but little cottages built of scree. The roofs were made of every kind of material. There was driftwood, rusting iron and even an upturned boat. Some were thatched with bunches of dry seaweed and others had tiles. From each roof a stone chimney was smoking in the grey light. When they finally came to a halt outside the captain's little cottage, snow had joined the wind, and it was bitterly cold.

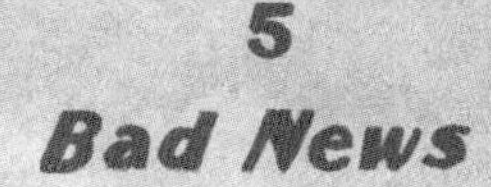

5
Bad News

THERE WAS A CLICK of the latch and the door opened. Silhouetted against the glow of lamplight was another shaggy seadog. She had a pup under one arm and another hiding behind her skirts.

'Uncle Hail!' exclaimed one little seadog.

'Hello, Blizzard!' said the captain, closing the door on the worsening wind. 'And hello, Snow.' The shy twin came out from behind her mother's skirts and greeted her uncle with a bow. She looked gravely at the strange white seadog perched on the captain's shoulders. 'This is a little stowaway,' the captain explained, lifting Sea Gem down. 'His name is Sea Gem.'

'Hello, Sea Gem,' they chimed together.

'Blizzard and Snow,' the mother seadog said, 'could you go and ask Percy if he would bring us some hot milk and cheese?'

When the little ones were gone from the room, the shaggy mother turned a desperate face towards Captain Hail.

'Thank the Great Blue Whale you're here!' she said, grasping him urgently by the arm.

'What's wrong, Flurry?' he asked.

'It's our own Frayed Rope. He is missing! He has not returned from his short journey this last week. He took some of the orphans back to their colony, but was meant to be here days ago. We fear the worst.'

The captain's eyes widened. 'Where is Frostbite?'

'My poor husband was beside himself with worry. He went yesterday to look for him, and he too has not returned. And now the weather has gone bad,' replied Flurry, wringing her paws.

'Be calm, sister, we will find them.'

Flurry nodded, and then, after pausing for a moment to collect herself, she turned to Sea Gem.

'Forgive me, I'm forgetting my manners. Come, Sea Gem, do sit down. I am Mother Icicle, but please call me Flurry.'

Sea Gem looked about for somewhere to sit, but there didn't seem to be any chairs, only colourful cushions in comfy piles.

The floor was covered in many woollen rugs which were decorated in intricate designs and edged with soft fringes. In the very centre of the snug was a stove a bit like the one from her own burrow, except that it was round. The captain sat down on a cushion and patted the spot next to him.

'Sit here, Sea Gem,' he said. 'We shall have a cup of warm seal milk, the creamiest and most delicious …'

The captain was interrupted by a scuffling sound at the door. It opened, and in waddled a penguin carrying a tray on his flippers. With careful steps which were punctuated with quacks and squawks, he reached the centre of the snug and placed it on the floor.

'Hello, Captain Hail,' he managed to say between a lot of other cheeping and squawking.

'Hello, Percy,' replied the captain. 'Meet Sea Gem.'

'Hello, Sea Gem,' said Percy with a little bow. Sea Gem was too surprised to speak and she turned back to the captain with a bewildered expression. Percy rubbed his flippers together and shifted uneasily on his leathery feet.

'What's to be done, Captain?' he said fretfully. 'Where can Frayed Rope be? I knew I should have gone with him!'

'Now, Percy,' said Captain Hail soothingly, 'it's pointless worrying today. The weather has closed in I'm afraid.' They all looked towards the tiny windows, which showed flurries of snow. 'Why don't you go back to the barn and try not to panic. I'm sure Frayed Rope will turn up soon.'

Percy turned reluctantly towards the doorway and then left the room, squawking anxiously.

When Percy had gone, Flurry sat down beside them on the cushions. The captain and his sister began discussing the disappearance of Frayed Rope in urgent tones.

While the shaggy seadogs talked in their strange accents, Sea Gem was thinking quietly. There was something about the name 'Frayed Rope' that seemed familiar. Then she remembered the bottle. Without disturbing the discussion the grown-ups were having, she retrieved her duffel bag from beside the door and rummaged through it. When she had found the bottle, she

pulled out the note and read it once more. She caught her breath when she read the pale writing *Fray* … something, and then ever so faintly the following word. She saw now that it most definitely said *Rope.*

'Sea Gem,' said the captain suddenly, making her jump, 'come and have some refreshments.'

'All right,' she said brightly as she stuffed the bottle and note back in her bag and rejoined them on the cushions.

Flurry handed her a mug of steaming milk. Sea Gem had never tasted anything so sweet and creamy.

'This is delicious!' she exclaimed.

'Why, it's kind of you to say so, Sea Gem. Seal milk dairy products are one of our important industries here in the Land of Ice. Now tell me, little one,' said Flurry, offering Sea Gem a plate of cheeses, 'why have you travelled so far?'

'Well …' began Sea Gem. But she didn't know what to say. She felt the many secrets pressing in on her, and wondered if she should just tell Flurry and the captain the truth, especially about the bottle and her daydreams. But she wanted them to like her, and if she told them everything, she was sure that they would think her very strange.

'I … ran away …' she began reluctantly.

Flurry's expression darkened. 'From your family?' she asked.

'I wanted to be in a cold place where the sun can't … hurt … and … I …' Sea Gem trailed off uncertainly.

'He's tired,' said Flurry sympathetically. 'I think we should all rest now. But when this weather clears,' she added, turning to Sea Gem, 'we will send word to your parents.'

Later, as Sea Gem lay in her bed next to the warm stove, she considered the strange case of the seadog in the note. But every way she thought about the facts, none of them added up. The message read *Lost*, but Flurry had said that Frayed Rope had only been gone a week, and Sea Gem knew it would take longer than that for a bottle to reach Foamy Bay. She calculated that the note must be much older. Whenever she thought about the note, she had a strong feeling of loneliness, but why? None of it made any sense. Slowly her thoughts returned once again to the most frightening part of all. If the seadog in the note was the same as the seadog she had seen lying on the ice in her dream … then Frayed Rope was badly injured! But Sea Gem didn't want to tell Flurry and the captain about what she had seen. After all, it was only a dream … wasn't it?

6
The Killer

SEA GEM SLEPT SOUNDLY. When she woke, it was to the soft clatter of clicking. Before she opened her eyes she lay in the drowsy warmth of her blankets, listening. The incessant clicking filled the little room, which was interrupted now and again by talking.

'You've dropped a stitch there, Chilly,' said an old, quavery voice.

'This pattern is complicated, Auntie Snowflake,' said another.

'If Great-grand-uncle Sleet can do it, anyone can,' laughed a younger voice.

Finally curiosity got the better of her and Sea Gem opened

her eyes. The scene before her was the strangest she had ever encountered. The little snug was full of shaggy seadogs and every last one of them was knitting!

They sat among the cushions clicking away with their knitting needles, letting long lengths of their colourful work drape across their laps and onto the floor. The baby seadogs she had met the night before were winding some red wool and getting into a terrible tangle. Sea Gem smiled and was sitting up to watch more closely when the door opened. It was Percy. He beckoned for Sea Gem to follow him.

When they entered the cooking-snug, Flurry sat Sea Gem on a cushion at the low table and served her a plate of plain biscuits and cheese, and a cup of warm seal milk. Percy squawked something she didn't understand and went outside.

'Good morning, Sea Gem,' said Captain Hail. 'So you've met the rest of the Icicle family.'

Sea Gem looked confused.

'The knitters,' Flurry added in explanation.

'Oh, yes,' said Sea Gem. 'Do they live here too?'

'Of course,' said Flurry. 'You didn't see them yesterday as they were knitting with another family on the other side of Blueberg. The bad weather prevented them getting home last night.'

As she ate her breakfast, Sea Gem took in her surroundings. Above her head a rack of dried fish hung by their tails. There was a black iron stove on one side of the snug and on the other was

a cabinet with a gauze front which held cheeses stacked in round wheels. Sea Gem regarded them with interest.

'Where do you make the cheese?' she asked.

'We have a dairy attached to our barn,' replied Flurry as she sat down next to the captain. 'We take the curds from the seal milk and use our own special recipe to make it into cheese. We store the wheels in the dairy and turn them each day while they cure.'

While Flurry was speaking, the captain was stacking supplies into a rucksack. 'I think I will try the eastern hut now that the weather has cleared,' he said. 'If Frayed Rope's in difficulties, that's where he'd go.'

'But that's in the opposite direction to the main penguin colony,' argued Flurry. 'Oh dear, if only we knew which way to go!'

'Now, sister, you mustn't fret. Why don't you do the milking while I finish packing?' said Captain Hail. 'Then we'll decide which direction I should search.'

'All right then, brother,' Flurry said with a sigh. 'Would you like to help me with the milking, Sea Gem? You can meet our milk-seal. But you'll need some boots. I've got just the thing.'

She opened a chest in the corner of the snug. Inside was a jumble of boots, and when she found a pair to fit, Flurry searched out some other warm clothes.

When Sea Gem was wrapped up and Flurry had collected a

bucket, the door swung suddenly open with a bang. Percy came rushing into the snug as fast as his short legs would carry him. He was waving his flippers about wildly, and squawking in a panic.

'Help!' he cried. 'Murderer on the loose!'

'What? Calm down and tell me, Percy,' said Flurry firmly.

But Percy held his flippers over his eyes and shivered.

'Percy!' Flurry continued, 'I can't help you if you won't tell me.'

But Percy was too upset to use words and, squawking loudly, he led the seadogs across the snow-covered courtyard.

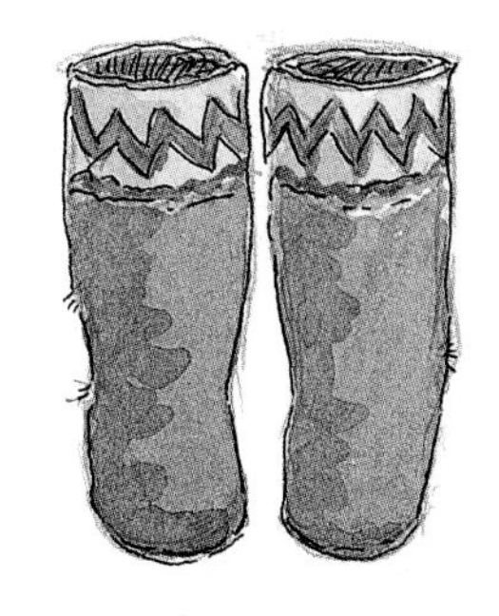

Not far from the Icicles' cottage was a large barn. A splintered hole showed at the base of the doors. It looked as if a wild animal had chewed it with sharp teeth. A sudden movement attracted their attention and they all looked up. Only metres away was an animal with a sleek spotted head, slithering in muscular movements along the ice. It reached a place where the ice sheet was broken, revealing the dark water underneath. The creature stopped then, and turned to face the seadogs with a baleful, black-eyed stare.

Sea Gem felt a sick lurch in her stomach. It was the creature she had seen in her dream; the horrible predator she was now sure had attacked Frayed Rope!

Flurry and the captain were silent with shock. Even Percy seemed to have turned to stone.

Then, the dreadful slayer fixed its gaze on Sea Gem and became very still. Suddenly it plunged back into the water. The seadogs were frozen in fright, unable to believe their narrow escape.

Flurry regarded the captain with terrified eyes. When she spoke, her voice was no louder than a whisper. 'The Killer is back.'

'That was a close one,' Captain Hail replied after a few long moments. Then he opened the damaged barn doors, and the others followed him inside.

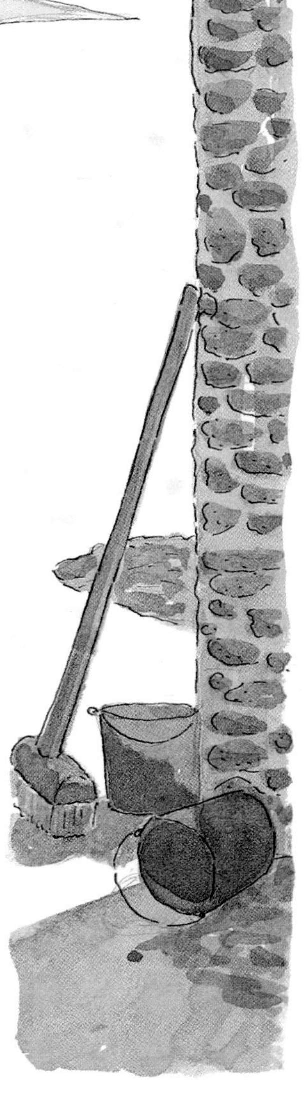

Underneath the warm glow of hanging lanterns, the whole place was full to bursting with baby penguins, who were cheeping loudly in panic.

'These are the orphans,' said Flurry to Sea Gem over the noise. 'We must check that none have been harmed.'

While they worked, Sea Gem's thoughts churned around and around. Should she tell Flurry and the captain that she had seen the Killer before? Should she tell them about her dream? One image kept returning to her mind. It was the look of fear and pain on Frayed Rope's face as he lay on the ice, and the spread of blood around his injured leg.

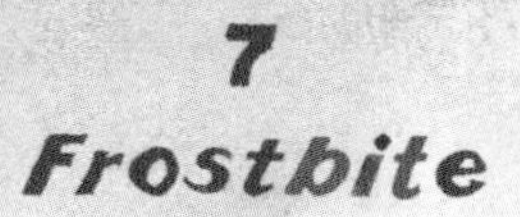

7
Frostbite

BACK IN THE COTTAGE FLURRY prepared a pot of squink. Sea Gem was quiet. She knew she should have told the Icicles the whole truth from the beginning. Now she had to speak up.

'Flurry …' she began haltingly.

At that very moment, Captain Hail returned from the barn with his toolbox. His face was tense with apprehension. He sat down at the table and gratefully took the cup of squink that Flurry offered him.

'I've fixed the door,' he said, 'but until the evil creature moves on, the orphans are still in danger.' There was a pause then, and in the small silence, Sea Gem took her chance to speak.

'Captain Hail,' she said softly, 'I've ... well ...' But the grown-ups' distracted faces frightened her and she asked instead, 'What exactly is a Killer?'

Flurry and Hail looked at each other and back to her again. Sea Gem could feel their uneasiness, but she sat up straighter in her chair and said bravely, 'You can tell me, I promise I won't be frightened.'

'Well, Sea Gem, the Killer is a leopard seal which has terrorised us for years. It's one of the most vicious predators of the South Pole and it attacks penguins with terrible speed. It leaps up onto the ice and wriggles along like a snake. It eats seadogs as well, but penguins are its favourite.'

'Why didn't it try to attack us?' Sea Gem asked.

The captain hesitated. 'Actually, Sea Gem, I'm not sure. When the Killer turned to face us I thought we were all done for.'

'Yes, Hail,' agreed Flurry, 'that was strange.'

They were all considering this when a noise sounded outside. Flurry looked up and then ran to the front door.

Before Captain Hail and Sea Gem had time to follow, they heard joyful barks and squawks from the next snug. Through the doorway came a very tired-looking shaggy seadog with Flurry and Percy at his heels. Eyes hollow with exhaustion, he sat down at the table and everyone waited in silence for him to speak. Several moments passed as the poor seadog pressed his eyes to stop the tears.

Sea Gem did not need to be told that this was Flurry's husband, Frostbite, returning from his search. She could also see that the news was not good. Flurry sat down and pushed a cup of squink in front of him. Frostbite looked at it blankly before drawing something out of his coat pocket and placing it on the table. It was a long, striped scarf with a fringe. Clearly marked at one end was a rust-coloured bloodstain. Flurry shrieked when she saw it.

'Frayed Rope's scarf!' she said, her eyes frantic with distress.

Frostbite stroked her cheek and said softly, 'It was the only trace I could find, but we mustn't give up hope.'

Sea Gem's heart hammered in her chest. She had travelled all the way to the bottom of the world to help Frayed Rope, and now was her chance. If she touched the scarf, she might be able to see where he was. She hesitated, her round eyes fixed on the dark stain. What would Flurry and Captain Hail think if she told them about her sight? Would they think she was a freak? Would they even believe her? She regarded the scarf with trepidation, afraid of what she might see. Maybe Frayed Rope was lying on the ice, his brow pale, his breath stilled and his dead eyes staring at the sky. Her thoughts whirled, and she looked up to see if anyone had noticed her distress. But they were not watching her, they were listening instead to the rest of Frostbite's sad story. It was Flurry's red-rimmed eyes which finally moved her to pity. She must be brave, she must try! With great effort, Sea Gem closed her eyes and placed her paw on the soft folds of the scarf.

Time seemed to go slowly, and she could hear her own breathing, loud and rasping in her throat. Then, a familiar whooshing sounded in her ears as the vision took shape. She was somewhere dark. Wood-lined walls came sharply into focus and then a stripe of grey light showed a seadog lying on a bunk. It was Frayed Rope! He lay still, his wounded leg dressed with a makeshift bandage. It was stiff with dried blood. Sea Gem then saw the gentle rise and fall of his chest as he breathed. He was alive! Behind him she could see a picture hanging from a nail.

It was a painting of a penguin standing next to a shaggy seadog. Then, the vision faded.

'Flurry!' Sea Gem said frantically when she found herself once again in the cooking-snug, clutching the scarf. 'Frayed Rope is alive. I think I know where he is. We must hurry as he is badly hurt.'

The Icicle family turned to look at her as if they had seen a ghost.

'What did you say?' they said, half afraid, half hopeful.

Sea Gem paused and looked from one shaggy face to another. There was no going back. Gathering her courage, she started to tell them all about her sight, beginning with the dream she had had on the boat.

8
The Search Party

SEA GEM FINISHED HER EXPLANATION by fetching the bottle from her duffel bag.

'I found this when my twin went out fishing. He loves fishing,' she added with a smile. Everyone was silent as this new information fell into place.

'You mean, your twin is a boy too?' asked Frostbite, puzzled.

'Great Blue Whale!' exclaimed Flurry. 'Sea Gem, you are a girl!'

Sea Gem smiled shyly as she handed Flurry Frayed Rope's note. 'I thought Captain Hail would think me more useful if he thought I was a cabin boy.'

As each member of the family read the note, Sea Gem prepared for the worst. She wasn't sure if they would shrink from her, or even more dreadful, laugh out loud. But Flurry's eyes were shining with unshed tears as she looked up from the note and gently took Sea Gem's paw.

'You mean you came all the way from your home in Foamy Bay to help our Frayed Rope?'

'Yes,' replied the little white seadog quietly. 'Only, I didn't know he would need it so much. When I found the bottle on the beach, I thought the seadog in the note was lost or lonely ... it was silly I suppose.'

Flurry opened her mouth to speak, but the captain interrupted her. 'Let us not delay!' he said, rising to his feet and shouldering the haversack. 'We must begin our search immediately.'

'He is in the place with the picture of the penguin and the seadog hanging on the wall,' said Sea Gem.

'The eastern hut!' barked Frostbite, dragging himself to his feet.

'No, Frostbite, let Hail search this time. You are exhausted,' said his wife firmly. Frostbite was too weary to protest, and he sat back down again.

'Do not worry, Frostbite,' Hail said, 'I will find him and bring him home.'

'Wait, Captain!' squawked Percy. 'I'm coming too!'

'And me also!' chimed Sea Gem, pulling on her woollen coat.

'Well, Sea Gem, I'm not sure ...' protested the captain.

'But Hail,' Flurry interjected, 'she has travelled so far … and you might need her power of second sight.'

Sea Gem beamed at Flurry and raced over to join the captain at the door.

'Aren't you forgetting something, Hail?' asked Flurry, who was holding out a small jar.

'Oh, yes, sister, of course!' he replied, dipping his paw into the jar and proceeding to smear the contents onto his face.

'What's that?' asked Sea Gem.

'Penguin oil cream to protect you from the sun,' explained Flurry as she gently massaged the cream into Sea Gem's fur. 'The sun in the Land of Ice is very fierce, and you must be extra careful with your pale complexion.'

Flurry then fetched Sea Gem a pair of dark glasses from the jumble of odds and ends on the dresser. 'You must wear these too. They will protect your eyes.'

The captain unhooked a pair of snowshoes from beside the door. 'These should fit you, Sea Gem,' he said, helping her to fasten the strange-looking contraptions to her boots. 'By the way,' he added when he had finished, 'I think you're even nicer as a cabin girl!'

Sea Gem was thoughtful as the little search party headed east, following the sun as it travelled low along the horizon. How wrong she had been. She had thought that the Icicles would not like her if they knew who she really was. She had thought that the sun in the Land of Ice would not burn.

Their path traced the shoreline, close to the floating platforms of ice. When she looked behind her, tall, snow-covered mountains loomed in the distance. Their giant shapes pressed up against the sky and Sea Gem shivered. Although the captain's presence reassured her, Sea Gem realised that she missed her own family. She felt a stab of longing to see her twin.

Percy waddled alongside, and occasionally, when there was a break in the ice, he dived into the water and overtook them with his fast swimming. Sea Gem turned to the captain. 'How much further is it?'

'Not far now,' he replied.

'The hut is around the next bend,' said Percy, who had joined them again. Behind the little party, just out of sight, a sleek head lifted out of the water. Its black eyes squinted evilly and it disappeared in a soundless splash.

As they walked, Sea Gem saw that the sky was growing darker and a few snowflakes began to appear. Sea Gem removed her dark glasses.

'I don't like the look of that sky, Sea Gem,' said the captain. He scurried forwards and Sea Gem ran to catch up with him, with Percy following as fast as he could.

Directly ahead of them the hut came into view. Its small, dark form was only just visible in the worsening snow and they all hurried towards its shelter. The wind and snow began to whirl around them, turning everything white.

A few minutes later, they started the short walk up the small slope to where the hut stood. Only now, the hut was impossible to see. Sea Gem looked around – she was suddenly alone.

'Sea Gem!' a disembodied voice cried. 'Are you all right?'

'Captain!' she shouted into the howling gale. In the next moment, his strong paw grasped her by the arm.

'Hold on to me!' barked the captain.

'But where is Percy?' cried Sea Gem anxiously, peering into the white for some sign of him.

'Don't worry about Percy,' shouted the captain over the noise of the blizzard. 'He loves this weather. He would have gone down to visit his friends at the other penguin colony.'

With a few more steps they arrived at the rough wooden door and the captain pulled it open. They stepped gratefully inside into the hut's relative warmth.

9
The Rescue

THE FIRST THING THAT Sea Gem saw in the hut was the little painting hanging from a nail on the wooden wall. It was just as she had foreseen in her vision. A soft bark sounded in the darkness. There was a seadog lying on the bunk, and he sat up and peered at his rescuers through the gloom. 'Frayed Rope!' barked the captain.

'Father?' he said in a hoarse whisper.

'It's me, Uncle Hail. Are you all right?'

'I think so,' Frayed Rope replied, his voice gathering strength. 'The Killer attacked me on the way back from the colony, but I got away. My leg is hurt.'

Hail gently inspected Frayed Rope's leg. It was hastily wrapped with a length of rag, but seemed to be healing well.

While the captain lit the lamps and set the stove alight, Sea Gem came and sat next to Frayed Rope. She couldn't believe that she was finally face to face with the seadog from the note. He was short-haired like her and he wore glasses of a strange style. They flashed in the lamplight as he bowed his head.

'Hello,' he said, 'I am Frayed Rope Icicle, and you are?'

'Sea Gem,' she said, smiling happily, 'Sea Gem Sandburrow.'

The captain rummaged in the rucksack and set the supplies on the table. When he had given the patient some water, he poured everyone a cup of hot squink from a flask. 'We'd better settle in for the night,' he said. 'We've no chance of getting home until this blizzard lifts.'

The travellers then shared a tasty snack of cheese, dried

fruit, pickled fish and crackers. When they had satisfied their hunger, they each selected a bunk and a pile of quilts to warm them. It had been such a long and exciting day that Sea Gem was asleep before she had time to think about it all.

The next morning, when the wind and snow finally died away, the seadogs awoke to a white world. Through the window they saw that right to the very edge of the sea was entirely covered with snow, and when they spoke their voices had a curiously hollow sound. The snow had made such a deep drift in front of the hut that when the captain pulled the door open, a huge mountain of snow came with it. Then, from behind the snow, a squawking voice was heard.

'It's Percy!' cried Sea Gem.

The squawks were followed by a lot of scraping and digging sounds. After some minutes, the doorway was clear. Several large penguins stood outside with Percy, and the captain stepped out to greet them. Sea Gem was surprised to hear that Captain Hail spoke to them in their own language. Then most of the penguins began to disperse. One of the birds waited behind with Percy, standing patiently beside the door.

The captain helped Frayed Rope to hobble outside wrapped in a blanket. Sea Gem watched in amazement as the penguin waiting with Percy lay down on his tummy. Frayed Rope sat on the penguin's back and the captain climbed up behind him. Then Captain Hail took off his scarf and placed it in the

penguin's open beak and held the two ends like woollen reins.

'Come on, Sea Gem,' said Percy, lying on his tummy like the other penguin, 'climb aboard!'

Sea Gem did as she was asked, and then threaded her scarf through Percy's beak. It was difficult to balance on his back, but she held fast to the woollen ropes. The penguins paddled their flippers and the creatures began to slowly glide down the gentle slope.

The freezing air ruffled Sea Gem's fur as they skimmed across the smooth white carpet. Frayed Rope and the captain raced ahead until soon they were only a speck in the distance. Percy started to play games, swerving to and fro, almost unseating Sea Gem. All of a sudden, he sank in a soft patch of snow and came to an abrupt stop. Sea Gem was thrown right over his head and into a powdery drift. Luckily she was unhurt, and she lay in the snow, laughing. As she stood up, she heard a loud splash. Only a few metres away, the spotted sleek form of the deadly Killer was snaking towards them!

Terrified, Percy leapt to his feet and waddled as fast as his legs could take him in the opposite direction, and the Killer, with muscular force, lunged after him. Sea Gem watched, horrified, as the seal opened its lethal mouth, showing pointed teeth just right for tearing flesh. The Killer barked, a nightmarish, scraping, growling sound which turned her blood

to ice. She knew she had to help Percy, so without any thought for her own safety, she scrambled towards him, sinking into the snow almost up to her waist. Percy was squawking and quacking. He kept running away, falling over, and then struggling again to his feet. With great effort, Sea Gem managed to pull herself out of the snow drift and onto firmer ground. She ran towards the two creatures and thrust herself between them, facing the Killer.

'Go away!' she shouted bravely.

The Killer stopped

still. Its liquid eyes were dark, and it held Sea Gem in its cold stare. Sea Gem stood her ground, but the Killer didn't lunge forwards to grab her with its sharp teeth. Unmoving, it continued to watch her. Sea Gem waved her arms suddenly and the creature jumped.

'Begone!' she shouted. The Killer cowered and then, with a growl, it began to back away from them.

'Look!' squawked Percy, 'I think it's frightened of you, Sea Gem.'

'Go away,' she shouted again. The Killer snaked, scrambled and wriggled, trying to put as much space between itself and the white seadog as it could. It was panting with effort and growling in fright. Then, an unexpected thing happened. The snow gave way from under the creature and, with a startled bark, the Killer fell in, disappearing from sight.

Sea Gem and Percy gasped in astonishment and ran to see what had happened. They very carefully approached the place where the seal had fallen in. To their surprise, the snow had been obscuring an enormous crevasse at least twenty metres deep. At the bottom was a sad scene, for even though it was a vicious creature, Sea Gem felt pity for its plight. At the base of the deep, icy chasm lay the dead Killer. Even from that height, they could clearly see the blood, which increased in a slow pool around its lifeless form.

Percy and Sea Gem were quiet as they skimmed back along the ice. Soon they could see the chimneys of Blueberg Hamlet, and when they entered the little town, Percy glided effortlessly between the cottages. Arriving at last at the Icicles' home, he used his flippers for a perfect stop.

10
Frayed Rope

THE DOOR OF THE COTTAGE swung open and Flurry threw her arms around Percy and Sea Gem.

'Great Blue Whale!' she cried, ushering them inside.

As they warmed up in front of the stove, Sea Gem told everyone what had happened to the Killer. She acted out all of the different parts, and even did an excellent impression of the deadly creature's growl.

'You should have seen her, Captain! She was very brave,' squawked Percy proudly.

'I'm sure she was, Percy. But why do you think the vicious

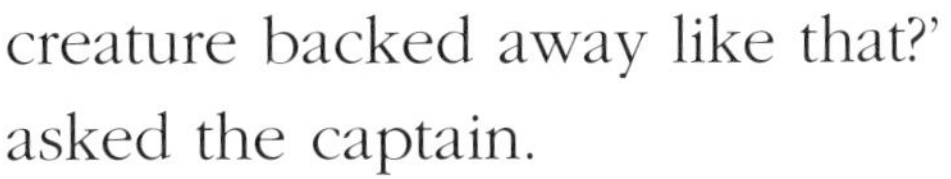

creature backed away like that?' asked the captain.

'I'm certain the Killer was frightened,' replied Percy. 'In fact, I think it was terrified of Sea Gem.'

'Maybe,' interjected Flurry, 'that's why it didn't attack us yesterday – it was petrified of your white fur, Sea Gem.'

Sea Gem smiled in surprise. If they were right, her white fur had been, for once, actually an advantage.

In the days that followed, Frayed Rope's leg healed.

Sea Gem spent many hours sitting at his bedside, entertaining him with stories. She was glad that Frayed Rope was safe, and that she had been able to use her power of sight to help find him. Maybe it wasn't so bad to have such an unusual talent.

Although Frayed Rope was out of danger, he had caught a cold. Flurry dosed him up with a tonic but it was more than just a sniffle. He seemed sad. Sometimes Sea Gem caught him staring out of the window. On one such occasion, she asked him what was wrong, but he shrugged, crumpling his handkerchief and pushing it under his pillow.

'Let's not talk about me all the time,' he said brightly. 'What about you? Why did you come all the way to the Land of Ice?'

Sea Gem fetched the bottle with its folded note. 'This is what made me decide to come,' she said, handing it to him. 'I found it on the beach.'

When he saw it, Frayed Rope sat up in bed.

'I felt you were lonely,' she added shyly, 'and that was why I came … to help you.'

'Really? You travelled that far … for me?' he asked, taking the note and looking at her with new interest. After a moment he added thoughtfully, 'That was very kind, Sea Gem … and you were right, you know.' He folded the note slowly. 'I was feeling bleak when I made this.'

Sea Gem smiled sympathetically, and then asked, 'Bleak? Does that mean "lost"?'

'Well, not absolutely … oh, it doesn't matter now,' he said, shoving the note into his pocket and turning back to face the window. As he rolled away from her, his handkerchief came out from underneath the pillow and fell onto the floor. Sea Gem reached down to pick it up, but as soon as it touched her paws, there was a whooshing sound in her ears. The vision surrounded her with sudden force.

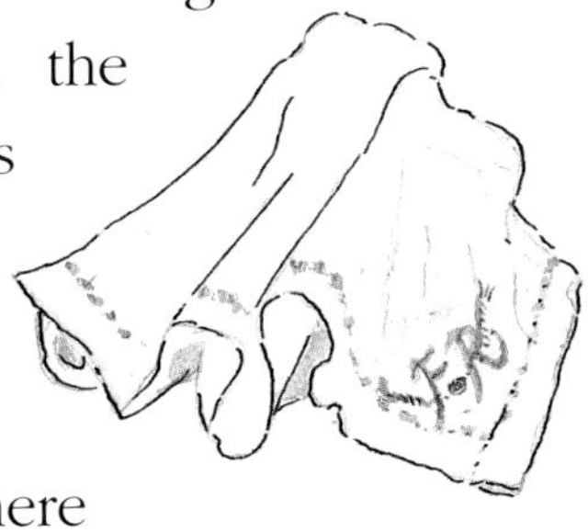

She was at sea, standing on the deck of a medium-sized sailing boat. A seadog stood at the wheel, looking up at the sails swinging uselessly in the windless sky. All around the sea was as calm as a pond, as flat as a mirror. Through a porthole she could see two babies sleeping soundly in a seagrass basket while their mother sang softly. There was a sudden shout, followed by a loud splash. The mother looked up in alarm.

'Grey Stone?' she called out.

Running up on deck, the seadog searched the boat for him. She leaned out to see if he had gone overboard, but what she saw was not her husband. It was a hideous sea monster with trailing arms. Its great eyes glowed evilly and its pale body moved under the water's surface. The poor seadog watched

helplessly as the horrifying creature cast its tentacles. The club tips made a loud crack against the cabin roof and twined around the mast with inexorable malice. Slowly, the boat began to tip over.

The vision changed at that point and this time Sea Gem saw a wild storm. The boat was smashed to pieces, and the flotsam was lifted up and down in the massive waves. The wind howled and sheets of rain lashed down. On part of the wreckage, one of the pups had managed to climb onto a splintered piece of wood. Still attached to it was a length of frayed rope. As he clung to the flotsam, the little seadog watched the seagrass basket, held aloft on the towering seas, drifting further and further away. He lifted his nose to the air in a desperate howl. His sister's little head poked over the basket's side, shivering with cold and fright, her yellow spotted nightdress dripping wet.

'Marigold!' cried Sea Gem in recognition as the vision faded and she was once more standing beside Frayed Rope's bed. She felt dizzy. The room whirled around her and she dropped to the floor in a faint.

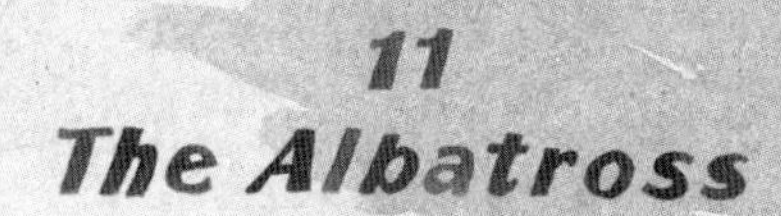

11 The Albatross

When Sea Gem opened her eyes, Frayed Rope was standing over her, his brown face rumpled in concern.

'Are you all right?' he asked kindly.

'A bit better,' Sea Gem replied, sitting up.

'Did you have another vision? Was that it?'

'Yes,' she said. The waves of dizziness had almost gone.

'I'll go and get you a cup of hot squink. Here, sit on the end of my bed,' Frayed Rope said, helping her to her feet. When he was gone, Sea Gem sat quietly, remembering the vision she had had.

Frayed Rope and Marigold were twins! She felt happier than she had in a long while and couldn't wait to tell them both. Letting Frayed Rope know was easy, but

Marigold was a very long way away. Sea Gem let her thoughts drift back to Foamy Bay and felt a pang of homesickness. She wondered if they missed her, too. She pictured Tumblegrass' cheerful brown face and realised that her place was at home with her own family. Even though she was so different from them, she was still a Sandburrow. The fresh knowledge washed over her and, as she closed her eyes to savour it, Frayed Rope returned with the hot squink.

Sea Gem took the cup, smiling. The reason for Frayed Rope's short fur was now clear to her, but it was more than that. Frayed Rope and Marigold were so alike, she couldn't imagine why she hadn't seen it straight away.

'Frayed Rope,' Sea Gem asked after a moment, 'do you know where you really come from?'

Frayed Rope sighed and, after a few moments, he told Sea Gem his story.

'Flurry and Frostbite found me at sea, clinging to a piece of wreckage. I was barely alive. They could see I wasn't a seadog from the South Pole, but they took me in and gave me the name of Frayed Rope like the seadogs of the north. I've always known that my parents had perished, but …'

'Yes …?' prompted Sea Gem.

'It's silly, but I have a hazy memory of a little seadog in a basket, lifted high on an enormous sea. Flurry told me that I was too young to remember, but I couldn't get it out of my

mind. That was why I sent the note last summer. I guess it didn't make much sense to you because the writing on the back is all washed off.'

'So that's why the note said "lost",' Sea Gem exclaimed, finally understanding. 'You were looking for your twin.'

Frayed Rope nodded and pulled the note from his pocket. On the back, Sea Gem could see the pale tracery of what once must have been Frayed Rope's plea for his lost twin.

'I really believed,' he added, 'that somewhere out there she was still alive, growing up in another family, like me.'

'But it's true!' blurted Sea Gem joyfully. And then she told him of what she had seen in her vision, and all about his lost twin, Marigold. When she had finished, Frayed Rope was silent. It was a lot to take in. At last he said, 'I was right! I knew it!'

After that, Frayed Rope had endless questions about Marigold and Foamy Bay. Sea Gem spent the rest of the day recounting all of the stories she could remember.

That night, the Icicle family were sitting around on the cushions in the knitting-snug. They talked about the amazing events which had joined the two families. Frostbite and Flurry kept looking at Frayed Rope, their faces alight with happiness to see him smile again. Blizzard and Snow climbed into his lap and listened to the grown-up conversation. They were discussing plans to get Sea Gem home to Foamy Bay. Of course, everyone had a different idea.

'What about going on Hail's boat next spring?' suggested Frostbite. 'He takes our milk and cheese north each year.'

'No, that's too long to wait,' said Flurry.

'What about the Great Blue Whale?' suggested Auntie Snowflake. 'You could meet at sea.'

'I think that's impractical,' said the captain. 'And too wet.'

'I know,' said Percy, 'an albatross!'

'Of course!' everyone agreed, 'why didn't we think of that earlier?'

So the arrangements were made for Sea Gem to fly home by albatross. By the time everything was ready, the days were shortening and the sea was starting to freeze.

The albatross arrived one morning, landing on the ice sheet. The beautiful white bird was enormous. The Icicle family bowed to him politely and offered him a basket of fish. Seadogs don't understand the albatross language, so Percy translated Captain Hail's directions. The helpful penguin kept the bird calm while the saddle was attached and the cargo strapped on board. When all was ready, it was time to say goodbye.

Frayed Rope came forward with a special package for Marigold.

'Please give this to Marigold,' he said with a bow.

'Won't you come with me?' Sea Gem asked.

'I would like to very much, but my family needs my help over the winter. I will come one day,' Frayed Rope replied.

'Marigold will be so excited,' said Sea Gem happily.

Each member of the Icicle family came forward to bow to Sea Gem, and she bowed back. Flurry presented her with a gift from the whole family. It wasn't wrapped, but folded neatly into a knitted bag. She pulled out the contents. The first item was a pair of sunglasses, followed by a jar of Flurry's own sun protection cream made from precious penguin oil. The last thing was the most wonderful of all. It was a knitted suit of the finest wool with its own hood attached. It was striped with the many colours loved by seadogs from the Land of Ice.

'It's a sun protection suit coated with penguin oil,' explained Flurry, 'so now you can swim or sail with your family in the sun.'

Sea Gem threw her arms around Flurry. 'Thank you,' she said. After that, Sea Gem climbed on board the albatross, and Captain Hail helped to attach the safety straps to her waist.

'Hold on tight,' he said, squeezing her paw briefly.

Then the great white bird spread its wings wide. It lifted off the ice, high and then higher. 'I will!' Sea Gem cried.

Epilogue

Sea Gem arrived home several days later on the beach of Foamy Bay. Old Cork and Blue Bottle wept loudly when they saw her. Although they had received a letter from the Icicles, they had wondered if she would ever return. They hugged her again and again saying, 'Thank the Great Blue Whale you're home!'

When the cargo was unpacked, the family exclaimed in amazement at the generous presents. There was a carton of cheese and butter, a sack of softest penguin down, a dozen bottles of penguin oil and beautiful knitted jumpers for the whole family.

The albatross was treated with a basket of fish and sent home with thanks and a letter for the Icicles. I'm sure Sea Gem began telling what was to be a long series of stories about her adventures in the Land of Ice. She would have done all the voices, imitating the strange accents of the Icicle family, keeping everyone entertained. Although I can't be absolutely certain, I have a feeling that her visions don't frighten her as they once did, and it's my guess that she often uses her powers to help her family. As for being a white seadog, I don't think she minds as much now, especially with her new knitted suit!

Although the Sandburrows were so happy to have her home, there is another family far away who miss her very much. How do I know this? Because it's me of course, Frayed Rope Icicle!

CAPTAIN HAIL'S

1. STEAMSHIP

A boat powered by a steam-driven engine. Skole (a special fuel made from dried seaweed and coal) is burned in the furnace to heat water and create steam. The steam drives the engine, which turns the propeller.

Chimney

wheelhouse

Wheel

MISCELLANEA

(or a Guide to LIFE in the Land of Ice)

2. LAND of ICE

A large frozen continent located at the South Pole (the very bottom of the world). Home of the shaggy seadogs, penguins, seals and the beautiful albatross.

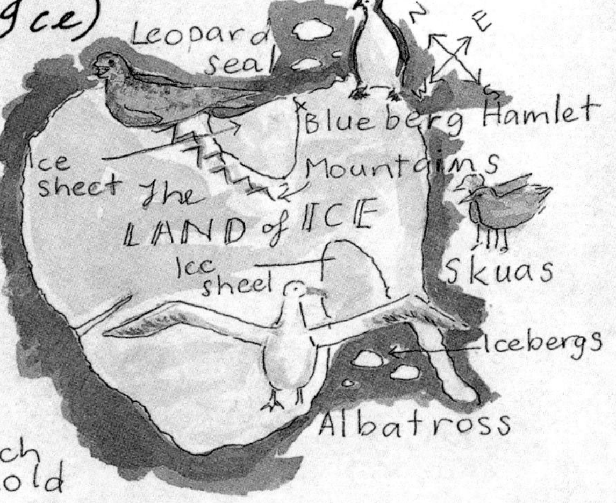

INDUSTRY in

1. SEAL MILKING -

Milk dairy seals are cared for by seadogs in exchange for their milk, which is the creamiest in the world. They are enormously fat creatures and love to eat large amounts of fish.

Mrs Weddell being milked

Milk seals sleep all day in warm barns

2. PENGUINS -

Seadogs and penguins are good friends. Orphan penguins are cared for by the seadogs until they lose their baby feathers. They are then returned to their colony. Seadogs extract penguin oil from a gland above the orphans' tails. This precious substance is used by seadogs for sun protection, waterproofing and medicine.

THE LAND of ICE

1. (a) DAIRY PRODUCTS

3 KNITTING

The feathers shed by the chicks (the softest in the world) are made into warm clothing, quilts and pillows.

Some GEOGRAPHY and

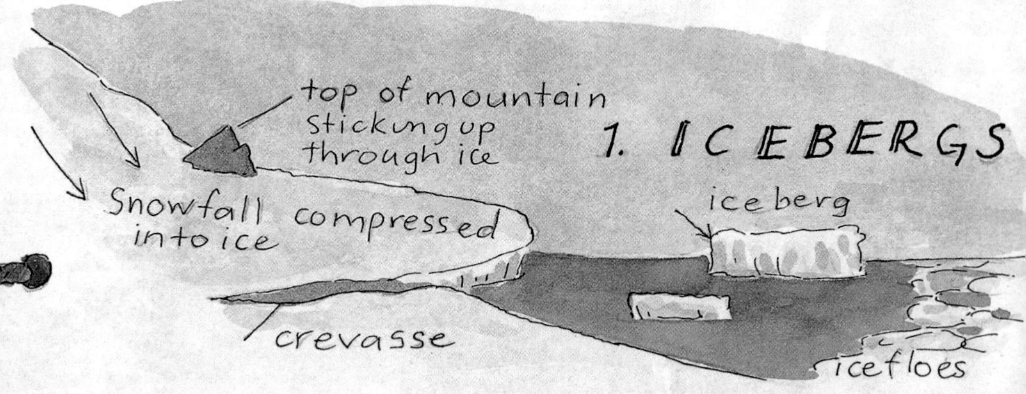

Icebergs are big chunks of compressed snow and ice which break off the ice sheet and slide into the sea, where they float. The largest part of an iceberg is under the water.

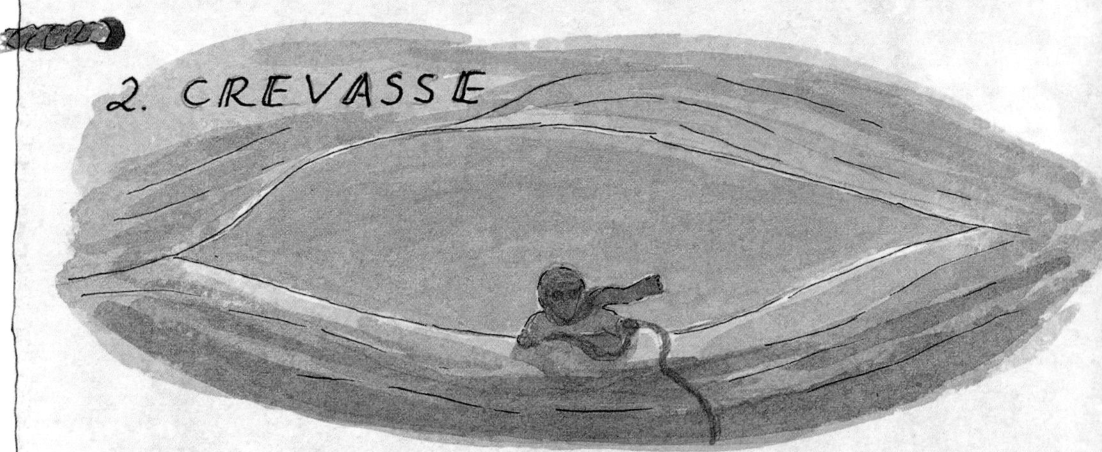

Crevasses are huge cracks in the ice sheet which are sometimes very deep. They are treacherous as they can be hidden by a covering of snow.

other interesting MISCELLANEA

3. SUN

The sun in the Land of Ice is very strong. It doesn't rise in the east and set in the west as it does in non-polar parts of the world. Instead, it tracks a course around the horizon from SSE towards SSW and then dips below the horizon. In summer it only stays down a short while before coming up again. In winter, it is the opposite and the land is dark most of the time.

4. SCREE

Scree consists of loose stones or broken rocks. Some beaches in the Land of Ice are composed of scree, which become exposed when some of the ice melts in summer. The seadogs build their houses from this kind of material.

5. FROSTBITE

Frostbite occurs on an extremity (eg, a paw) when it gets so cold that it freezes. This kills the tissue and parts of it turn black. These 'dead' parts sometimes have to be amputated.

For my parents

Thank you everyone, especially Anna McFarlane, Brianne Tunnicliffe, Imogen and Kitty (proofing, advice), Thomas (shadows), my brother David (cover), and friends with cups of tea. Thank you a thousand times to Stephen, the best husband ever!

Visit: www.seadogs.com.au
First published in the UK in 2007
by the National Maritime Museum, Greenwich, London, SE10 9NF

www.nmm.ac.uk/publishing

First published 2006 in Macmillan by
Pan Macmillan Australia Pty Limited,
St Martins Tower, 31 Market Street, Sydney

ISBN 978 0 948065 88 0

1

A CIP record for this book is available from the British Library.

Typeset in 13/18 pt Garamond by Seymour Designs
Jacket design by Seymour Designs
Printed in China

Penguin Oil